who's ready to play?

and lots of other questions

Kane Miller
A DIVISION OF EDC PUBLISHING

Who's splashing whom?

Who's upside down?

Who's swapped places?

Who's ready for lunch?

Who's changed color?

Who's taking a nap?

Who's hiding in the snow?

Who's pooped?

Who's found a friend?

Who's showing off?

Who's had a baby?

Who's ready to play?

Who's afraid of mice?

Who's looking fierce?

Who's looking the other way?

Who's who?

Dog

Panda

Horse

Tortoise

Kangaroo

Elephant

Cow

Hippo

Chameleon

Lion

Polar Bear

Cat

Duck

Snake

Tiger

Peacock

Owl

Pig

Whale

Rhino

Zebra

Giraffe

Crocodile

Monkey